Purchased from author Elaine Govern
at Riceville - Oct. 11, 1985 Friday

We drove thru Riceville enroute to Cresco
for dinner at Stan and Gail Kvam home —
then on to Decorah for Luther College
Homecoming. Bob also was honored at
Friday evening banquet where he was
presented a Distinguished Service Award
from Luther College. Orlow and Juanita
Walstad stayed at our farm Oct. 10 & then
also drove to Cresco and Decorah with us.

My father Esler Clarence Dirks and my
mother Lillie (Dresselhaus) Dirks owned and
operated Dirks Ice Co. at Decorah from Mar. 1, 1928
to 1949. On March 1, 1928 we moved to 904 Fifth Ave.
in West Decorah. This house was right on the Oneota,
or Upper Iowa, River, from which the ice was cut
and stored in the big ice house. The ice was
packed in sawdust so the cakes would not freeze
together.

Ice Cream Next Summer

ELAINE GOVERN

Photographs by *Lawrence J. Pitzenberger*
and *Elaine R. Govern*

Library of Congress Cataloging in Publication Data

Govern, Elaine.
   Ice cream next summer.

   SUMMARY: While watching his father cut ice for
the summer, a 1908 Iowa boy learns a little about
controlling his impulsiveness.
   [1. Iowa—Fiction]   I. Title
PZ7.G745Ic   [E]   72-13349
ISBN 0-8075-3533-8

Second Printing 1980

Worzalla Publishing Company
Stevens Point, WI

Michael hated having his picture taken. He had to stand so still for the photographer.

It was hot and sticky, this Iowa summer day. Michael's stiff collar was too tight. It pinched his neck. The thick stockings and high-top shoes were too hot.

Pa frowned and said, "Michael, stop pulling Laura's hair."

And that was Michael's problem. He did things without thinking, things like pulling his sister's hair, throwing rotten apples, teasing the chickens. He never thought of the trouble he made.

Michael tried to remember things that were more fun than having his picture taken.

He thought of earthworms in the garden and of horses. He thought of the new electric light bulbs in his father's general store.

Michael's hair was damp from the heat. He thought about the coolest place he knew, the icehouse. He thought about something cool made with ice — ice cream.

He remembered how Pa had gone with the sled and horses to get ice from the lake. How Michael wished it were winter right now!

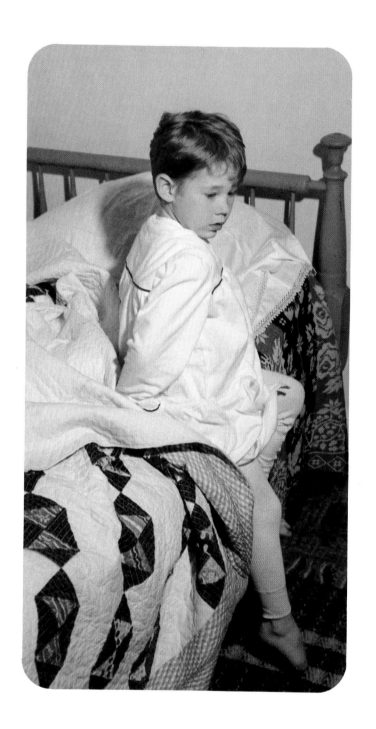

Winter came. The snow fell, and the photograph in the parlor was Michael's only reminder of hot summer days.

There was a stillness to the December morning when Michael woke. It was the stillness that comes when it is very cold, when animals huddle quietly together for warmth, and snow scrunches underfoot like squeezed popcorn.

Michael sat up in bed. He looked for his puppy Tag. He was not in his box in Michael's room.

The puppy must have been shivering, Michael thought. Maybe he had bumped down the stairs on his fat bottom and short legs to the warm kitchen.

After breakfast, Michael ran into the store.

Pa's store was in the front, and the family lived in rooms in the back.

The big store stove was shiny on the outside. Inside the blue flame burned the black coal to gray ashes.

On a cold day like this, Michael would have to carry out many buckets filled with ashes.

There would be little time for Michael to play with Tag or the toy horse and cart he'd been given for Christmas.

Yesterday he'd eaten the last piece of the orange he'd found along with the nuts in his Christmas stocking. He had made his orange last almost a whole week by eating it little by little. That was longer than Laura had made hers last.

Everybody in the family helped in the store. Laura and Michael had many chores to do.

People came to the store to buy groceries, nails, cough medicine, or woolly socks. Pa liked selling hardware and talking about the town news with the men. Ma enjoyed selling lace and thread.

Michael loved the store's smells: kerosene, molasses, coffee, and leather, all mixed into one big smell.

Michael went to the door of the store and looked at the falling snow. It fell on the wooden porch and walk. To Michael it seemed to be waiting for him to come out and slide.

With a bang Michael let the door slam. He was out sliding on the slippery wooden porch. He pretended he was a flying machine.

Then the door opened. "Michael!" his mother called. "Come in. It's too cold out here with no coat. Stop and think." She hurried him inside.

Michael knew he was in trouble again. Pa looked down at him from his high desk where he was writing numbers.

"Don't do things without thinking," Pa said. "Go and dust the shelves and counters."

Michael liked dusting. It was a good chance to look at the things for sale. He always ended his dusting at the curved glass candy case. The cheese had a glass cover, too, but Michael liked candy better than cheese.

He looked at the rock candy, the lemon drops, and licorice, wishing he could have a piece.

Michael wondered if tomorrow would be as cold as today. Pa had said the first cold days after Christmas something special would happen.

Next morning when Michael woke, the stillness and coldness made him sure. This was the day.

He left the warmth of his patchquilt and ran to Laura's room. Jumping on her bed, he said, "Laura, wake up! I think it's the day."

"Will they let me go, too?" Laura asked.

Michael didn't answer. He knew girls weren't allowed to do boy things. Anyway that's what Pa said.

Michael went to the washstand that held a big bowl and a pitcher of water. The unheated upstairs was so cold there was ice on top of the water in the pitcher.

With care, Laura and Michael broke the ice and poured water into the wash basin.

The icy water tingled their faces and made their fingers numb. Michael started to grin at the thought of dumping cold water on his sister.

But the sound of Pa's footsteps going down the stairs changed Michael's mind.

Michael hurried. He didn't want Pa to leave him at home.

This morning he didn't wait for Laura to button her shoes and take the rag curlers out of her hair. He pulled on his own clothes and ran downstairs.

When Michael came into the kitchen he knew it most certainly was the day. Pa had on his work shirt. Ma was in the pantry. She had on the skirt she wore when she worked in the store.

"Good morning, son," Pa said. "This cold spell will last three or four days. Time enough to cut all the ice from the lake we'll need for next summer. You can come along."

Michael smiled with happiness.

"But, Michael," Pa warned. "It is dangerous when we're cutting ice. You must use your head and think."

As Michael put on his coat, Tag looked up with big wanting eyes. He was so soft, and he begged to play.

Michael thought, "I wish I could play with Tag and go to the lake, too." Then without thinking any more about it, he bent down and picked up the puppy. He stuffed him inside his coat.

Laura was watching. She shook her head. "Don't, Michael," she said.

But the door closed, shutting off Laura and the warm kitchen from Michael, Tag, and the bitter cold. It was too late.

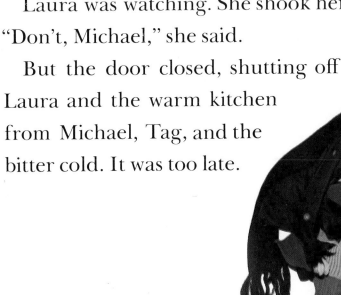

"Uncle Jim will meet us at the lake," Pa said while he covered Michael with a big laprobe.

Pa never noticed the bulge under Michael's coat, and the boy didn't mention the puppy.

Pa put the large iron ice tongs into the bobsled. He lifted the crosscut ice saw with the big teeth into the sled. The saw had a long curved end with a wooden handle.

Then Pa climbed in, picked up the horses' reins and called, "Giddap, Duke, giddap, Dan!" And the big horses started off.

The cold that stung Michael's cheeks could not touch Tag. "Just don't bark," thought Michael. And Tag was quiet, lulled to sleep by the gliding bobsled runners squeaking over the crusty snow.

Michael was not asleep. Set in a blue sky, the sun was a golden ball. The snow glittered. The cold made the horses breathe hard.

At the lake there was Uncle Jim waiting for them. Pa took off his long fur coat. The shorter coat he wore underneath was easier to work in.

"Stay in the sled," Pa warned. "I heated the soapstone on the stove at home. Put your feet on it or your toes will be frostbitten."

There was so little snow that the ice did not have to be scraped before cutting. The water beneath made the smooth ice look gray-blue. Uncle Jim took an ax and chopped a hole in the ice.

Michael could see the ice was about a foot thick.

Starting at the hole, Pa sawed two lines.

Then every two feet he and Uncle Jim hit the ice with a metal tool called a cake splitter. A block of ice floated free.

Using poles, the two men pushed the blocks so that they could reach them.

The men lifted the blocks of ice out of the water with iron tongs.

They loaded the ice on the bobsled.

Watching from the bobsled, Michael wondered. Were there fish in the open water? He forgot about Tag and jumped down to see.

The puppy fell to the ice. The little legs tried to stop sliding. They were not strong enough. The open water was very near. Splash! Tag slipped into the icy water. Michael shouted, "Tag! Tag!"

But in an instant the water and the current pulled the puppy down, and away, and under an endless ice blanket.

It all happened so quickly that Michael could only kneel by the hole in the ice, big tears running down his face.

Then Michael felt a hand on his shoulder. Gently his father turned him away from the empty hole and lifted him into the sled.

It was quiet on the cold lake. No one said a word. The men finished loading the ice.

Michael and Pa started back home to the ice-house. Looking up at Pa's face, Michael knew that Pa was sorry, too.

Pa said nothing on the long trip home. It was not the time to scold.

The late afternoon sun, low in the winter sky, was a falling star flashing behind the black trees. The warmth had gone out of its glow. And the warmth of Tag's furry body was gone from under Michael's coat. The blue shadows cut across the path. It would be sunset soon.

Michael's face burned. The tears froze on his cheeks. Inside he felt a lump bigger and colder than all the ice Pa could ever cut from the lake.

When the horses reached home, Pa hugged Michael and told him, "Go inside."

There was no time for anything more. The ice had to be put in the wooden icehouse. Soon it would be too dark to work, and there were no lights in the icehouse.

The ice blocks had to be packed in sawdust to protect them from heat next summer.

Laura met Michael at the door.

"Tag is gone in the dark water under the ice," he whispered.

Laura was quiet for a long time. The hurt feeling entered her heart, too.

She thought of saying gentle words like "I'm sorry." She thought of comforting words like "Pa will get you another puppy."

And she thought about saying "I told you not to take Tag. If I could have gone, I would have been smarter."

But Laura didn't say any of those things. She was quiet and shared the hurt feeling. None of those words would help Michael. At last she did say, "Ma is going to give me a candy stick. I'll ask her to give you some, too."

Then some of the coldness inside Michael melted. A sister's love was softer and warmer than any puppy.

Later that day Michael looked at his sister and smiled. He would not pull her hair any more.

Winter went by, and so did spring.

Summer came. Michael's two front teeth were missing. He was taller. His mind had grown a little in understanding. Pa did not have to talk so often about thinking before doing something.

One day Ma took sugar and eggs and cream and mixed them together. She added vanilla. Pa brought ice from the icehouse in a wheelbarrow.

The children helped Ma pack chips of ice and salt around the can inside the ice cream freezer. At first it was easy to turn the crank. Then it was harder and harder and Ma helped Michael.

When she opened the freezer, Ma told Michael, "You can have the first taste."

Michael put a spoonful of ice cream in his mouth. It was cold. He thought about the cold day when Pa had cut the ice.

Some things,

    like ice cream and growing up,

        have to be taken slowly.

Ice Tools

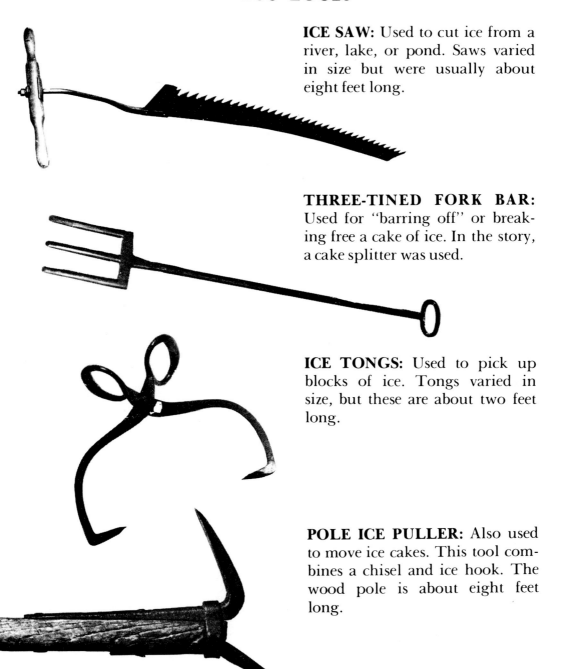

ICE SAW: Used to cut ice from a river, lake, or pond. Saws varied in size but were usually about eight feet long.

THREE-TINED FORK BAR: Used for "barring off" or breaking free a cake of ice. In the story, a cake splitter was used.

ICE TONGS: Used to pick up blocks of ice. Tongs varied in size, but these are about two feet long.

POLE ICE PULLER: Also used to move ice cakes. This tool combines a chisel and ice hook. The wood pole is about eight feet long.

CRESCENT or ICEHOUSE SAW: Used to separate frozen ice cakes.

SIEVE SHOVEL: Used for shoveling ice. The shovel was made to prevent scooping up water.

HAND ICE PULLER: Used to move a cake of ice. The handle is of wood and six inches long, the iron hook is five inches.

ICE ADZ: Used to shave off uneven tiers of ice.

A Note About This Story

Imagine a country store closed in 1907 and not reopened for sixty years! This store, ready for visitors, stands in the Forestville State Park in southeastern Minnesota. Original merchandise lines the shelves, and the big nickel-plated stove still occupies the place of honor.

The availability of this store was a lucky coincidence when Elaine Govern chose 1908, the last heyday of the general store, as the time for the story she planned to illustrate with photographs. This was the era just before the common use of electricity, before the automobile, before life became urbanized.

At first, Mrs. Govern simply intended to show children how food was handled before modern refrigeration, but the story soon grew beyond giving information. It became a picture of family life in a time when an emphasis on closeness and responsibility sometimes collided with a growing boy's impulsiveness.

To achieve the authenticity Mrs. Govern desired, the settings, costumes, tools, and action had to be in so far as possible genuine. She, her husband, son, and niece became the family pictured; her brother was the photographer for most of the scenes.

In manuscript form, the book helped Mrs. Govern earn her master's degree in library science from the University of Northern Iowa. Now as a picture book, it gives a warm glimpse of the past.

The author appreciates the assistance she received from these persons and institutions:

The Forestville Store in Fillmore County, Minnesota, State of Minnesota Natural Resources Department and the Minnesota Historical Society

Jacksonville Historians Club, Jacksonville, Iowa, located at Five Corners on the old military road to Fort Atkinson, Iowa

Waterloo Museum of History and Science, Waterloo, Iowa

Mitchell County Historical Society, Osage, Iowa

Mrs. Peg Gorman, New Hampton, Iowa

Mrs. Mazie Moss, Riceville, Iowa

Mr. and Mrs. L. B. Pitzenberger, New Hampton, Iowa

University of Northern Iowa Drama Department, Cedar Falls, Iowa

Malcolm Price Laboratory School, Cedar Falls, Iowa

In addition, she wishes to thank Margery Anonson, William Biederman, Leonard Crawford, Joan Diamond, Mary Elliott, Steve Engelhardt, Jay Foster, Clyde Greve, Peter and Shawn Govern, Dolly and Laura Gorman, Monabelle Hake, Emmett Henley, Agnes and Bill Hines, Charlotte Lawton, Verna Leichtman, Elizabeth Martin, Mary Lou McGrew, Evelyn O'Bryne, Steve Pitzenberger, Neva Sheehan, Caroline Rubin, Della Taylor, Mrs. Leonard Theis, Luther Thompson, Martha Timmerman, Genevieve Woodbridge, and Joyce Zoulek.

Locations for the photographs include the countryside around Riceville, Iowa, the Forestville Store, and homes or buildings made available by Mrs. Gorman, Mrs. Moss, and Mr. and Mrs. L. B. Pitzenberger.

Other persons mentioned modeled, provided antique articles, professional services or assistance.